M000079639

Dirty Daddies

The Complete Storybook of the Hottest and Most Forbidden Erotica Collection of Father Affairs with His Daughter and other Fetish Secret Stories to Quench your Thirst for Taboo Stories

Part-2

Samantha Tillery

Stories

Dad Fucked My Best Friend 5

William Shared His Wife with M 24

I Had a Wonderful Night with a Best Friend of My Daughter 41

Elizabeth Had a Great Time with Her Father's Best Friend 58

Sex with the Big Black11 Inch Cock 75

Dirty Daddies

© Copyright 2021 - All rights reserved.

The content contained within this book may not be reproduced, duplicated or transmitted without direct written permission from the author or the publisher.

Under no circumstances will any blame or legal responsibility be held against the publisher, or author, for any damages, reparation, or monetary loss due to the information contained within this book. Either directly or indirectly.

Legal Notice:

This book is copyright protected. This book is only for personal use. You cannot amend, distribute, sell, use, quote or paraphrase any part, or the content within this book, without the consent of the author or publisher.

Disclaimer Notice:

Please note the information contained within this document is for educational and entertainment purposes only. All effort has been executed to present accurate, up to date, and reliable, complete information. No warranties of any kind are declared or implied. Readers acknowledge that the author is not engaging in the rendering of legal, financial, medical or professional advice. The content within this book has been derived from various sources. Please consult a licensed professional before attempting any techniques outlined in this book.

By reading this document, the reader agrees that under no circumstances is the author responsible for any losses, direct or indirect, which are incurred as a result of the use of information contained within this document, including, but not limited to, — errors, omissions, or inaccuracies.

Dirty Daddies

Dad Fucked My Best Friend

Johnson was a little upset at seeing Katrina's costume. Her
mother died three years ago, and Katrina arrived at the
university. He was surprised when he tried to hold back his
tears when he thought that he was living alone in his house.
"Dad, I want to ask you something," Katrina said, stopping
packing. "Here is Linda," she said. Linda was Katrina's best
friend in high school. Linda was a beautiful girl, but her
house was full of problems. Police often visited Linda's
apartment. Violence, alcohol, and drugs raged in his home.
But Linda managed to stay away from her parents and other
family members. "The situation in her house has recently

worsened," Katrina said. "Since I won't be here much, I thought Linda could use my room," she continued. Johnson thought for a moment. He knew from Katrina's face that he did not want to say no. There is nothing wrong with that, he thought. I don't want to stop at all, he thought. "Linda needs a break from her family," she added. "Call her and ask her to come home tonight so we can talk about it," she replied.

Katrina called before hastily finding her cell phone. "Thank you, Dad! That means a lot!" Katrina. Linda moved after Katrina moved. Johnson told Linda a few lines at home, and she agreed. It was a little strange that Johnson was the daughter of someone else in the room. But Linda was excellent from the start. He attended classes at a local university and had two jobs. When I went out, I was doing yoga and other exercises underground. Johnson is surprised to find him - down underclothes and support - a sports bra, with her rigid body, because she is exposed to pussy rubbed slope to the south clothes "I'm just trying to stay fit," he said when he noticed a smile. "Good," he said, before he went to the basement there with his erection, he recalled that he intervened after the death of his wife. , When they began to have a comfortable procedure, so they often sat and talked with pills in the kitchens. He must admit that for a young woman in her twenties, she had a good head on her shoulders. His social life was quite simple, but it was his choice. She wanted NIE that romantic troubles would catch her attention because she was determined to succeed in this. Her worried family convinced her to take control of her own life, and not just adapt her life to the expectations of others. "No one can tell me how to live my life, and this is my business," he said. Over time, Johnson saw Linda, a kind of replacement for the girl. It looked like Katrina, but Linda wore only linen and a bra. Her inappropriate thoughts began, especially when she saw her leaving the bathroom completely naked. I did not know if he knew that he was at home. He stopped in the room and picked up a small towel that covered his head. She could drink all her beauty while the cold air strengthened her nipples, while her energetic, happy breasts lay on her chest. Her flat stomach led to a bush that was neatly trimmed. He had a beautiful little dick on his hot legs. Her legs were gorgeous. Then Linda leaned in the middle and saw wet lips on her clit. When he entered his room, Johnson stayed there with a big erection. He could not sleep that night and thought he heard something strange. He left his room and entered the room to conduct an investigation and went to Linda's door. It sounded like a weird but familiar drone. When she heard Linda laugh, she knew exactly what she was doing. I liked His member hardens immediately. It was early morning, and it was calm. She could hear everything that Linda did with every quiet look, the sound of her play as she stimulated her clitoris. He heard her lying on her pussy with a bent bed when she fell for joy.

For the first time in several years, Johnson pulled out his cock and began to beat him. She imagined kissing Linda, seeking her climax. She thought about sucking her beautiful breasts and shaking her young and mature ass. I heard that Linda's actions intensify when her main point draws near. She adapted to her rhythm and listened to her scream with a scream. I knew that he led it that way. He finished his first series of years and felt that he had no end. He was then surprised that he was standing with his cock at Linda's door, listening to his orgasm while his load was being processed. He returned to his room in silence and was cleaned. A week later, she was surprised when Linda came home a little earlier than before. "I thought you were working tonight," he said.

"No, I need rest; I work all month," he replied. "What are

you planning?" He asked. "Just a movie after buying

Chinese food," he replied. "Are you worried if I go with you?" he asked. "Not at all," he replied. "Well, just give me a minute to get dressed," he said, running up the stairs and touching his pretty ass in his washed, skinny jeans. "Calm down," he told his cock as he grew up. Linda got worse when she went down the stairs in tight shorts and a loose shirt. He tried not to notice this while eating, but closed his eyes and brought the dishes to the car. Then she heard him cry. "The pipe evaporates me," he said with a smile, returning to the living room with a wet sweater. The fabric was now glued to her balloons with protruding nipples. He opened a bottle of wine and loaded a DVD before sitting on the sofa. At the beginning of the film, Linda got up and said it was cold. Then he went into the closet and returned with a blanket. Cover it with a blanket before you hit it. She laid her head on her shoulder and hugged her even when she was surprised. He dropped the page a bit while filming. She

16

moans closer with her hand on her hip. He struggled to concentrate on the film and put his hand on the waist to make it a little denser. At that moment, he laid his hand directly on his lap and began stroking his cock. "I knew you listened to me last night, and it excited me," he said, eating his erection. "I was thinking about you," he said, bringing his face closer to him. Her lips touched and shared a passionate kiss with tongues. He examined her body with his fingers when he put one of his fingers under her shorts and found that they were naked. He exhaled and controlled the bay. The fight put pressure on her daughter's best friend and took off her shorts before she buried her face in her pussy, she screamed and screamed, licking her pussy.

Then he put two fingers and licked her clit. His whole body was stretched, and his head fell. "Yes! Oh yeah! "- cried he, reaching the top. She lowered her hips to her face during an orgasm. Johnson then took off and quickly took off his clothes. He grabbed his cock and slowly stroked it. He lay on the sofa and hugged him before taking the cat into a kitten and looking into his eyes. For a while he moved his hips to get more of his cock, and began to bounce. She muttered, taking off her sweater and swallowing her swollen chest. She took her ass and joked about her cheeks. He moved his finger in the direction of the crack and joked on the buttocks. Then she took his glasses and began to fill his cock. He shouted, muttering uncontrollably. Damn! Two were near the top. It and leads to all four floors. She reached for her buttocks to lay her doggy style on her cheeks. She shot a dick at him and started to strike him when he tried his sperm to extract. He jumped a finger and squeezed it in his tight, ready-made ass. She lowered her head and began to rub her lips.

Johnson hid his penis and finger as deep as possible, and they jumped to the climax. He felt the cat milking his cock, and could no longer bear it, emptying the eggs in the pussy. That night they took her several times and taught Linda to suck his cock. He also got his morning. The next morning, he opened his eyes, and Linda had already left the house. He felt better than for years. His colleagues noticed the change, deceiving him. She didn't see Linda that night, but she knew that she had two working classes. She did not want to become obsessed because a young woman fought for success in her life. I hope to see her tomorrow, but she did not understand because she left early and returned when I was already in bed. He felt that his daughter's best friend was ashamed of what had happened, although it was a resurrection for him. The next day, Johnson went to work early in the hope of meeting Linda at home. She did not want to feel embarrassed because her family was already worried. When he returned home, he was listening to his room. He called him and let him in. "Good?" he asked. "Of course," he replied, but avoided eye contact. "I wanted you to know that

I decided to go home," he said. "What?" He asked in surprise.

"If this is the last time ..." it did not end, tears filled his eyes, and his cheeks flushed. "My father is right, and I am a prostitute," he said. He leaned over and took his face in his hands to see his eyes. "Don't let anyone tell such a lie," he said. "They have achieved a lot, more than millions will do in their life," he added. "You are not a prostitute, and you never think of yourself," he said, before leaving her. Her emotions were so strong that we trembled and disappeared. He suddenly felt ashamed and foolish. For a moment, they stood in awkward silence.

Then Johnson turned and left the room. He went to the kitchen. He looked out of the kitchen window until he heard a faint sound behind him. She was Linda. He opened his mouth to speak but put a finger to his lips to silence him. They hugged him and realized that they loved each other, appreciating their proximity. Her lips tightened into a soft kiss and itchy when her tongue reached the jaw line before touching the blade and curling her lips. She broke off the kiss to ask her if she wanted this but again touched her finger. Smiling, she laid her hands on her hips and shook her. He opened and pulled out. He stroked his fingers, hardened during touch. She lied when she kissed her head. She looked at him and grabbed the man between her lips. With the tip of the tongue, resulting in a hole in the urine, breathing, groaning. He opened his pants and put him on his feet to catch their balls, slowly stretching his cock. He sucked both eggs, and this could not last long. He felt it when he slowed down and kissed her again.

Then she swallowed more of his cock in her mouth and sucked deeper as she chewed on his balls. He broke fingers in her hair and grabbed her ass to pull deeper, as she knew that she would become tall. He groaned when he filled his mouth with hot cum and swallowed it. She helped him return and kissed him before completely removing his pants. Then she took her to her room and brought her to bed. They kissed passionately and deeply for several minutes. She got up and took it. She received her and began to kiss her skin. She knew that her breasts and nipples were soft, but she released her and kissed her on the stomach. He laughs, letting his belly button slip. He opened his shorts and bowed to her body with thick kisses, not taking a single step. She took off her panties and kissed her lower abdomen right above her pussy. She creaked, trying to make him touch his mouth. She took off her underwear, went out and smacked her ass, and then ran her tongue over the gap. He stood up and pulled her to him. He felt an erection increase between his cheeks. Then she sent him and cut off her bra to free her young and happy chest. He took her hands and returned to admire her body. Her eyes were full of hunger and sexual expectation. He stroked her body with his hands and then stroked her breasts. She covered his hands when she pressed hard against his chest. They passionately kissed him as he held firm breasts between his fingers. She grabbed one of her nipples with her mouth and sucked him until she bent her knees and fell onto the bed. He continued to suck on his balloons and laid a hand on her pussy. He softened her lips and found her clit. He joked about him until he reached his peak. Then she moved to the entrance to the pussy without penetrating. He ran and hit when it bothered her. She let go of her breasts and entered her pussy. She was open between her legs, and her pussy was dripping with juice into the slit of his cock. The view was beautiful. With a strong desire, she turned her hips and pressed her lower lip in anticipation of what would happen. Johnson took a long time to hit his head between the hips. He ran his tongue over the gap and extended his lips with his thumb before licking a wet hole. It increased the speed of his attention as he shook his head back and forth as she pressed her hips to her face. She jumped to her chest and trembled louder when she looked and trembled with happiness.

Johnson did not stop there. When her daughter's best friend came to her senses from her height, she turned her stomach and pressed herself against him. He poured her cheeks and licked a hole. Then she put her finger on her pussy and added one when she had a bite again. He returned it to its place and concentrated on his clitoris. She licked, stroked and gently sucked and rubbed her pussy to open it. She made a plum finger from her pussy juice on her ass. Now she ate her delicious pussy and kicked her ass, screaming. Finally, she grabbed her head and pressed it to her pussy as she lifted her ass and destroyed it during her orgasm. Then he picked it up, wrapped it in arms and legs and kissed it passionately. "This is your pussy, fuck me!" He said, grabbing his hard cock and pushing him to her pussy. She quickly pressed her cock into his cock, and her pussy reached his cock when she started stroking. They filled the room with sighs, the sound of a vibrating bed, and the beating of their body. She whispered again and again in his ear and invited him to hit her. She came closer to his body as she circled and screamed with the muscles holding his cock.

Dirty Daddies

William Shared His Wife with M*e*

When does your breast size change? I always thought that breasts were just breasts. They had women. The boys loved him. Not much and neck is the neck. All of us, like men, have dirty thoughts, but we can all keep our mouths shut until the time comes. I grew up as a gentleman. As a 21-year-old black man, people automatically think that you are a cowardly gun. Sometimes the boys look at me and say: Watson, you are young, you have a sound body and these severe eyes. You can beat the girls every night. Yes, of course, I am also a person who cares about his motives. A woman who never asked to be touched her. And I have only the edge or jugs of women considered as a real to me are interested in, if you know what I mean. The perfect gentleman, yes, that's what they said about Watson.

My position was questioned when I met Mary. I met her by chance while I was for a snack at night. The woman behind me begins to speak from scratch. "What do you eat, healthily?" He said with a smile and a smile and looked at the healthy twinkly snacks, lemons, and potatoes. "Oh, yes," I laughed softly. It is a weekend that I have to spend a bit. "You must, and you must take care of yourself."Just when I returned politely, I saw the strangest thing; this beautiful white lady was lying on her huge chest." She looked decent and friendly, like a thirty-year-old mother with a long brown border and sunglasses. His eyes were tender and attractive, a pleasant smile, but when he let his body rest, he saw two full breasts, one large chest, and one base. Hairstyle with short sleeves with a view of the great white shirt "... Hmm ..." I do not think that if you go directly to their huge jugs, it's me, I'm not sure about the power or comments. I didn't mean to sound rude, but what can I say if we both know what they know? All I think is "shit!" He laughed: "I know that they are long." "Well ..." I was embarrassed. "I did not say. I said. "The cashier looked uncomfortable for me, but the girl looked really ... interested in the word. A woman with big breasts bowed her head. "So, today's holiday. Can we go for a long night game?"Is this a question or an explanation?" "

They both laughed and shamefully shook their heads. "Of course, we can celebrate." Why did she just play with this woman because she showed a little tear? I saw many women in these suits, but then my mind was not so dirty. Why did I suddenly grab his chest and pretend to invite him on a date? "Yes, it was nice talking to you," he nodded politely and walked a few steps away from the big horns. I had the opportunity to free her, but something made me keep talking to her. I know what it was — two good reasons to support to continue the discussion.

I quickly received a receipt from my treasurer and played to catch up with the store. "Well, party, ma'am." She looked at me and those huge breasts; I do not smile as soon as I see my eyes. "If you have nothing better than eating Twinkies on a Friday night, you should celebrate it with us." "Oh, yes?"Not only my husband and I" "Oh, I understand." It sounds frustrating, but I tried to get it right. She was married and unavailable. Why is she still looking at these breasts? Maybe because they were so shocked that I could not imagine why they were running so. But the idea is that women with big breasts aren't all porn stars unbearable? The gray car stopped, and the little white man bowed his head out the window.

"Hi." "Hello," the woman said to her husband. I will try to convince my friend from the supermarket by celebrating with us. "Oh, yes?"Of course, but, look, I do not want to overwhelm you look like a good couple. "Milf and her husband laughed."Yes, my husband is a good companion ..." "No, no, no," I said blushing. "I just wanted to say that you have two good things. I don't want to be the third motorcycle, that's what I had in mind." "Well, come in. If you go home," said the gentleman, but impressive. "I'll be leaving soon." "Hi, buddy, little meat chicken," I laughed. "Good." "Yes, but not the place where I cook?" "Yes, of course," laughs the little bald man. As if I could take you to the race. "Yes, but you can have a gun."

"Find me," the woman said, reducing her unit to approval. "No weapons, no lies." I smiled and was speechless. I finally understood what they were talking about, but I was afraid to say it first. Blacks should never be the first to offer an orgy. I know, "Lady, I don't think she should look for her," I laughed. Not with playful hands. "Try it with me." "Yes, find it," said the man, smiling. "Do not carry weapons, I promise you." She said that as the time before take-off shirt and exposed her breasts, the biggest pair of fuses that I whenever seen.

There, a woman stood in front of me and showed her large eggs with pointed nipples and large pictures. I laughed, "You completely robbed me." "Yes," he said with a smile, taking off his shirt. "So, how do we think the same way?" I smiled like an idiot when my husband opened the front passenger door for me. I burst into Mary's living room with fear. I was not accepted, but I agreed to visit her house. After what I have gathered, they invite "some" men, mostly blacks, to their room, especially after a few weeks. I was never a hedgehog, but, man; huge breasts were what I could not get rid of. "You don't have to do what you didn't want to do," Mary reminded me when she said it was. William's husband sat comfortably on the couch and looked forward to what would happen. Sit next to him, and I next to her. "So, we are talking about you or me?" Mary said with her hands on her hips and her large puppies, who dared to touch her. I usually avoid the topic for myself and choose it later. "Well, tell yourself." "What about me? What part of me?" He said with a smile. "Hm, so if you don't care, if I ask you, are you wrong?" "Believe it or not, they are real; they always upset me when I was growing up. I thought about breast reduction for a long time, but then I met William, and he convinced me to keep going." The right choice, I told William he said yes.

She smiles. "So I think that everyone who teased gave me a fetish for them, now I want to show myself to the public, I usually go out without a bra." "That means yes." She already remembered my next question. He pulled his shirt down and put beautiful breasts a second time on exposure, this time with daylight. Oh my god, they were incredibly round, natural, and wild, with perfectly shaped nipples. "I looked at William, who ultimately accepted me with a bow. I put my hands on her chest and cried with joy. "Don't take them alone," he said, feeling my reluctance to be greedy. "Touch my nipples."Wow ... "I said that I gently squeeze the nipples until they become hard."Do you like it?" "I whispered when my laugh disappeared, and I was excited right now."Yes, I think so. "I wanted to resign but grabbed my wrists to stay."Do not stop. Tell us how you feel. "

I was very excited, like her, and her husband looked at us with approval. I really could not say what I was thinking: "Tell me what you think," she smiled and looked at her nipples, which was always a pleasure. "Think ..." "Say it." "I like your big boobs. I think ... it would be nice to put my dick between them. "Yes?" "Do you like it?" "No. Maybe you can show us how," he said nervously. She leaned back to pick up her blouse. "Take your dick off, Watson." "Oh ..." I smile sadly. "I don't know." "Come on, and you don't have to do anything, I just want to see it." Unfortunately, I laughed, but recorded it in person. "Come on, I showed you yours, and you showed yours!" "Well ..." I laughed, hoping that

William would support me, but I helped him. "Well, let me do it, be silent and smile." She knelt and put her arms around me. He lowered his head to my knee and began to squeeze my fly. "Wow ..." "Quiet," assured that it was not in vain that I had no time to look at the big black cock that was hidden. "Ahhhh ..." I am embarrassed, excited, embarrassed that my massive erection was hot, playing with her breasts. "How long is she, dear?" asked William. "Hmmm ... I would say eight inches." She looked at me, still wearing the glasses of this sexy teacher, put her lips on my cock and gently kissed him. Before I could resist, I did it again, sucked hard, and gave a warning, as if saying: "Don't challenge me, you idiot." Yes, I had to be an idiot to prevent this! Maria began to milk my head very slowly, leaning on the sofa and in the perfect position for me. I had to sit back, let go and smell the smoking mouth of this milf. "Mmm ..." he said, pulling him out, but stood by the tree. "Do you like white women sucking your dick?" "Oh, yes ..." Since she was next to me, and I was happy, it was more like a bow. But hell, it was fantastic and better than before when I say this. Maybe it was just the size of the big jugglers that made this thing so enjoyable. "He makes sure to slip to the side, past the bar, and under the sensitive head, that I was the most important event. He pulled my mouth out of my cock and caressed it more and more. Everything is good and damp, right? Why is it, "I know not," he said shyly. I think you need to wait and see. "He caresses and sucks me until I feel completely straight and throbbing." Like, "Oh ... "But ... this is not what I want," he says sarcastically," I know how children think. She holds big breasts together and invited me to my amazing mommy. "Oh, my mind is reading."

"You are all the same." She complained and got up from the couch to make sure that she followed her. He sat on his knees and held her chest and back, so that you have enough space for them to be bored well. "Oh Lord," I knit, leaning on my dick with her huge white chest. "Um ... I like the big black dick in my boobs." He tried to clear me from top to bottom, but caused friction. Her saliva was already dry. "Give me some grease," he told William. He answered after a few seconds, digging, grabbed the bottle and vomited. He grabbed it with one hand, alright! And it opened. "Good evening, good loss!" "A worthy goal," he said with a smile, lowering light grease in his hands. "Oh, yes ..." I flew, and I watched her leave her big breasts sweet with me, and I watched all the time. Dear Jesus, I still remember the bright light of your bags, oily, slippery to hell and ready for a good trip. He again greeted my cock on a colossal chest and pressed my cock to his flesh. This time with their bloody breasts is, I am very easy to and when I want to kiss a cat or mouth. I struggled with the need to get up or close my eyes, because I felt so good that it was almost painful. But I managed to keep my eyes open, glued to her chest and looking helpless when she led my cock and screamed mercilessly. I like it. Let the little man cry. You control and hit a rocket. I looked at her husband, who always looked crazy and fucked with these married breasts. You do not look, but you look at her carefully, as if large breasts destroyed his wife. "Oh yeah!" I screamed and tried to do it at the last, last, last and last this incredible moment. "Good, yes, Watson, you are fucking like a monster! Touch the white chest!" "Yes!"

I cried as if I had a fucking with Watson. These breasts were big monsters, and I killed them like a bitch! I came back and turned the member hard and fast in and crushed her breasts, so when I tried to light a fire. "Yes ... Maria, big boobs ... Did I call you at school?" Yes, it was rude, but, my God, it was a big revolution. "Yes," he replied, it looks so cool when I get their fucking jokes with big boobs. "I thought so ... in the supermarket ..." "Yes? Fuck these boobs?" "Yes!" I screamed, and I still hit the crushed melons, a few strokes more than a run. "So, I showed you. I know that you like black big white breasts. "Dead bitch, take my sperm!"Where? "He asked in flames in her chest!" William said and jumped off the couch to see him better. "Ahhhh! I ran!" I let go when the semen flew over his chest and chest and rolled over his stomach. "Yes, give me black sperm!" I gave it well. I was very afraid of my chest. She started and embraced her shiny breasts and made sure that she pulled an even load on her chest. She rubbed my male lotion into my chest and sent me and my husband with a deep sigh of ecstasy. I'm pretty sure that William is wearing pants. I know that I came. Everywhere there was evidence of Mary, who used every drop of sperm to adorn her milky white breast. No, this is not fair. It's not fair to laugh at women with big bats. And not because the woman got divorced, that she was a prostitute. But hell, except for political correctness, it's nice to kiss a vast chest.

Dirty Daddies

I Had a Wonderful Night with a

Best Friend of My Daughter

Thomas Taylor was surprised. She wondered if she had been

angry since she was king an hour ago, and now she was in a

mess. He was 36 years old and a business manager. He

always managed to maintain his rank everywhere, but what

happened changed everything. Many of Mila's daughter's

friends met at home on Saturday afternoon. They planned to

attend a party organized by another girl as part of their

diploma. This was not the first time the girls were with

Thomas because they served as the basis for their various

activities. They were talking and joking around the pool, and

Thomas was there too. The girls laughed at their presence

because they treated them with respect and attention.

However, in recent years, she secretly admired their adult

bodies when they became impressive young women.

Katty was Mila's best friend. He looked innocent and relatively calm. He had imagined them for many years and had already removed cherries from his dreams. This Saturday was Katty. It wasn't, and they tried to call him but received a voicemail. Then they decided to go to the party, because it was too late. Thomas was already excited to spend the day with the girls, waiting for them to leave to relieve tension. He got used to it after his wife left him about five years ago. Thomas was tall and always took care of his body through regular exercise and exercise. As soon as he searched the Internet for a good story about sex, he heard someone knock on the door. To his surprise, katty stands there with an innocent smile on her face. "Honey, you just left," he said. "I slept and did not see the time," he replied. "Mila was desperate to call you," she complained. "Yes, I forgot about it in another room and did not bring it with me," she answered disappointedly. "Okay, give me a minute, and I will take you there," he suggested. "No, Thomas, okay, I don't want to go." He replied: "I'm tired, and I want to use the pool." said she.

"This is the first time you apply for a pool permit," he said, admiring every inch of his slim body. She felt an earthquake flow through her body when she realized she would be home alone. "I would be grateful if my application accepted." Katty noticed Thomas's distinctive look when he was seventeen, and he was already in development. She was not interested in her appearance today. "You can use Mila's room," Thomas replied, looking around slowly as he entered the house. "Thank you, it's not that far," she replied, entering the room, and waving her cheek made her cock tight, and a few minutes later, Thomas went to the visitors' bathroom, where she had the best view. Katty bit her chest, bikini of different colors, and the top helps to cover, and the bottom knife was very low. Crossed their flat stomach and their small triangle and covered his steps. He felt a strong desire to smell a kitten and just kick back in Mila's room and found that Katty's clothes were folded on a bed with cotton sub-wear on the battery; he had a cross in his clothes and the heady smell of the vagina in his cock. Growing up, she put on her underwear on her head and pressed a branch to her nose when she began to stroke his cock.

When Thomas was about to shoot the sperm, Katty entered the room. "Oh my god! Thomas, you are fucking like my daddy. I'm sorry!" Katty called out, turned, and left. Thomas was surprised and sorry that it was just an accident. Still, it happened so unexpectedly and quickly that they did not even know if this happened at that time, I knew that he would apologize. Again, more importantly, he had to find out what he was thinking about embarrassment - he had already arrived in the room, asked the guest and went to the pool - looked at Katty, and asked where he was, she knew that she was at home alone in a swimsuit can leave went up, and I

went to so because her eyes could not believe it when she

saw Katie, to lying in the middle of the bed and saw a puddle

after a few seconds after the impact, could say: "Katty, I'm

sorry for what happened ," - he said, "Thomas, do not worry,

what you need ," I would not go into the room without

knocking", - he said. "In the end, this is your home, and you

will break," he continued, pointing to the design of the

trousers. "I mean, it was wrong to smell your underwear," he

said. "No quotes! I mean, it's normal for a person who smells

a bit like a cat," he replied, looking carefully at your

language and reactions in the body. "And I'm sure this is not

the first time," he said. "How normal, and how do you know

this is not the first time?" "Thomas asked in

surprise."Thomas, forgive me, but I saw a lot of stones with

dirty clothes, and for several days I go around the house all

day," I admitted with a smile. Oh my God! Does Mila know

this? He asked, though himself. I was glad that what

happened in Mila's room didn't hurt him.

But he still had a half-naked young woman in his bed, and he did not know what would happen, because it was clear that his daughter's boyfriend was plotting evil, but he did not know how far he would go. Would let go "I think that all men smell like underwear and that all the girls wear dirty shorts," he said. "I'm sure Mila is no exception, but now this is not my problem," he said, looking directly at the store, which became more transparent with Thomas's whole heart. "My current problem is visible, and my father interrupted me in the middle of a serious problem", - said the seller. "And now, this is torture for you." When he heard Katie call him dad, Thomas had a cold feeling that he had a bloody relationship with his daughter. "Well, I was ready to turn when he stopped me, and he could not leave for a second," he answered, looking at his desire to be half-naked. By the way, Katty was late to Mila's house because she had a plan, and this incident greatly facilitated the situation. "Dad, what can I do for you?" he asked playfully. "Let me see your father. I want to see him," he said, taking the boxes and lowering them before kneeling before him. His cunning member stepped forward and touched his hand. He turned his fingers and looked at him." for so long, "he said. Thomas knew that he was seven centimeters long. When Katty described a lot of Dix, he knew right away that this was probably the first man. She licks her head from the tail and between her lips. She began to suck and lick. "? How is this child?" asked Tom. "It's salt," answered the reason -. This is "Suck hands over the top," he said when he got it right. Thomas was taken apart only when she felt his tongue lick at the bottom of the rim. "Put it in your mouth," he ordered. He saw his mouth with a large chunk and wrapped his fingers around the rest, suffocating from enthusiasm. The movement with a hot tongue around his tail and a beautiful face that came and went was too much for Thomas." I will explode, "He shrugged and lifted a member in his mouth. He felt his cock freeze, stretch, and threw a rope.

Katty made a funny and funny sound when he shook his head. The first line of light sperm landed on her chin and lips, and the second touched her cheek, nose, and face in front of her. He got her last chest, leaning back. He took sperm from her breast and his face with his hand as he ran his tongue over his lips. He felt sperm when he laid a hand on his face and looked at Thomas. Then he licks it. "Not bad," he said. "I will swallow next time." He looked at the sperm from the chin to the chin, and his legs were restored, despite the considerable peak. She could not believe that a beautiful young woman knelt in front of him and licked sperm from her hand. Katie got up and went to bed, and Thomas sat next to her. He put his hand on his bare thigh and began to move him along his barefoot. She took a deep breath when she tapped her empty channel and stared at him. Slowly, she stroked the inside walls of her pussy and laid a finger on her little clit. Her legs were automatically extended and she was wet. He felt the feminine aroma of fresh pussy, and his cock became hard. "Dad, I'm still a virgin!" He said. "Do you want to stay that way?" he asked. "No!" She answered immediately, because that was the reason for her late arrival. "I want you to take my cherry. Be my first father!" He explained this while lying on a comfortable pillow. Thomas leaned over the girl and laid his body on himself as she spread her legs. The crab snuggled up to him with a sweet and warm hill from the bay.

Katie moved her hips up and down to rub her pussy against Thomas's erection. He licked her breasts, and the young woman listened happily. Her nipples were hard, and her tongue movements were excellent. This was the first time he felt this. She stroked my point of view and squeezed my cheeks as she stroked her hands as she moved between her hips. Katie closed her eyes and gently picked him up. He used his fingers to part his lips and stick his tongue into him. Katty wrapped her legs around Thomas's back and pulled him to her chest as she moved her hips, clasping her head in her arms to invite him. The young woman was thrilled and knew exactly what she wanted. Thomas was glad to welcome him. She uttered a loud voice when she felt her tongue licking her hard clit. Turn your head hard against her pussy and spread her legs so that she can be with her tongue in her pussy while she alternately stimulates their clitoris. She began to wave her hips, and Thomas continued. She felt that it was at the top when she started to raise her tongue.

"Ohh ... yaaaaa ... Aaaaaaaaaaaaa ", - he complained to Katie when his first rag touched her young body and pulled the clitoris."Dad, please stop," she moaned, resting her head on her hips. But her slender body betrayed her as she continued to rub her mouth across her vagina. She heard, finally, in the course, but he continued Thomas's head in his hands. He had his mouth open and his eyes closed, after he took the air and kissed her on the lips so she could taste their pussy juice. His hard stone tail pressed against a wet crack, and the contact was so excited that it fell. She wanted to be fucked by her best friend's father. Thomas moved his hips to stretch a member on soft moist lips. He reacts strongly with a sigh. While he was with passionate kisses, he broke his thigh with his leg and took his cock between his lips and vagina. "He pulled that - something close to the front and outer lips around the head. Thomas looked deep into his eyes Katty and realized that he was ready for the cherry suggestion of her father's best friend. He lifted his feet and leaned on his knee so that the thigh lay on her small breasts. She lowered her hand and extended her lips when Thomas buried his head in his crab in the boy. narrow pussy . "I'm almost to the baby.

It's enough to loosen if you have muscles," he warned.

A tear formed in his left eye, wiping Thomas with his thumb. He passionately kissed her, grabbed her ass, and pulled her. He struggled with pain. "I can stop if the pain is too great for you," he said, although he died to attach the entire member to his chest. He used his wet thumb to gently rub his clitoris, and despite his slight pain, he felt an increasing menopause. As soon as it got too hot, Thomas squeezed his finger slightly, but Katie raised her hips to bring back the strong feeling she had expected and ignored the pain in her pussy. As a result, he struck as hard as he could, tear his flesh from the psalm and tearing it apart. The young woman was surprised to find that most of his cock was buried in his narrow canal. Mouth and eyes were very open. "Baby, he's inside," he whispered, wiping tears from his eyes. "It hurts, but now I'm a real woman who loves," he muttered. Thomas started his hips in slow motion to settle, and the cock's head moved deeper with each hit. Katty was wet when she began to answer. She slowly turned her hips to follow her rhythm as she exuded a soft, regular, and pleasant moan from her mouth. "My God, Dad, I need everything in me. He's doing well," Thomas whispered in his ear. He threw his dick in tight pussy and made two thugs shake. He cried out in surprise and happily banged his head. , she grabbed her legs behind her back. She competed from her vagina before entering again. She pressed her legs tight to her back and sighed.

Thomas felt his balls boiling violently, and he did not know how to get his dick out of the narrow tunnel until he reached his peak. "I'm close," he said, looking at him with wide eyes. "Dad, you want this. I want you're cum in my pussy," she replied. "Do you like sex?" he asked with a smile and shook his head: "So get ready, baby, because I will fuck you hard until your pussy is filled with my sperm," he warns, lifting his body and completely falling on him. The intensity of her movements shook the bed when his muscular body hit hard on the thin body of thin Katty. She hugged him tightly. "Aaaahh ... Ohhh ... Thomas ... yes," he cried. She tied her up and screamed, squeezing a big cock out of a beautiful little pussy. She pressed her nails in her ass, panting. Then it exploded to a massive peak, and Thomas decided to take action. The highlight that Katty attracted , she wanted to use several times to release sperm in her pussy. "Oh my goodness," like birds semen, waving and filling the pit around the bird falls, falls out of fruit and crack the back of Katty. "Dad, what happened?" he asked.

"Well, honey, you just made your first highlight with a cock," he answered impatiently. "Wow! I never thought that I could find in the two soon," he said sadly. "Girl, this is just the beginning," a- he said. "They will be in the top ten before your friends come back and let me come," he added. "Really

I did ? She asked me a diploma. With a big smile, "Dad, from now I am very party to lose," he said in jest. "Of course you do," replied - she was in the arms of a weapon. She sleeps long in bed with a happy smile.

Elizabeth Had a Great Time with

Her Father's Best Friend

"I returned!" Elizabeth cried, although she knew that no one cared. They came back to the winter holiday from their native university and would like to spend a vacation with their parents. It was very cold outside, and it took about five minutes to remove all layers of tissue from her cramped young body. She was tall, with healthy breasts and dark brown hair that covered her shoulders with matching eyes. When he took off his clothes, he did not see Richard enter the room. He was his father's best friend for several years and was considered a member of the family. "Go! So Richard, I have been waiting for you here for two hours," he continued. "Parents, you went a few days ago and come back today," he said. "But his flight was delayed due to weather conditions, so I was asked to greet him and keep him until he returns," he added. "Well, it's a shame that they are stuck there, but I would like to make your company", - he said. "I talked for hours about my car on the radio," he added.

Elizabeth knew that her cat needed a company. She has not been tired in the past two weeks since her boyfriend left college to visit his family. She fucked her before she left, but two weeks had already passed. Richard was sexy too. He was tall and had a well-built, stretched body. His hands were strong, and his black hair was silver, and his green eyes were sexy. Her lips were full, attracting Elizabeth's attention as she imagined kissing her lower leg. She turned out to be her father's best friend since she was a teenager and fantasized about him. "So sweet, what do you want to eat?" he asked. He thought he asked for a piece of meat, like a tail, but stopped. "Why don't you surprise me?" He replied. "Well, bring your luggage to your room and take a shower during dinner," he said. "You can be back in forty-five minutes." "Yes, sir," she replied in her childish sarcastic voice before climbing the stairs to her room. Richard had a loud voice, and Elizabeth enjoyed dominance. That is why he obeyed without resistance. She went to her room and immediately threw her bags. He put his foot on the bed, warmed himself, and stood in front of his father's best friend, thinking about his body without clothes and smell. He imagined that he ordered him to kneel and put sex in his mouth, pressing his hand to the back of his head. Sometimes he ran his fingers over the covers, tightening his throat. He had fun in his bed and forgot to cook dinner. Right now, he heard Richard's footsteps in his head, but her pussy was so good that he couldn't stop stimulating him. Then he suddenly heard the steps stop, looked at the door, but made sure that he did not see it. He wanted an adult to enjoy the show when he saw it. Richard was harder to hear. He even adds some tricks to wake him up. "Oh, Richard, yes! Take me when you get stronger! Burn fast. Then Richard suddenly opened the door. "I clearly said that you should spend forty-five minutes," he says, "Because you seem stubborn, you are getting a lesson," he continued.

"Go and kneel," he ordered. He obeyed without hesitation. "Put your skirt on your thick ass," he ordered in a dominant tone. Before he saw him, he began to twist his ass without warning. It hurt, but he loved it. He could not control himself when he started to rise and tried to chew on his swollen clitoris on Richard's leg. "What the hell are you doing?" he asked an old man with a rich voice. "Take you away," he continued. "Look at my pants, who's going to clean up?" he asked. "Sir, I'm sorry, I will do it for you," he replied firmly. "Let me clean your pants," he suggested. Richard grabbed her hair and pushed her away. "You have to lick it now so that it does not get dirty," he said. He looked at Richard and slowly sat down his tongue to clean his pants. When a mature man was satisfied with his work, he took out his hard cock and rubbed his lips. Then he used his swollen head to hit him on the cheeks. "Now open your damn mouth," he ordered in a loud voice. "Yes, sir," he replied, remembering how he had deceived him, and sarcastically said the same answer. She liked to swallow a member deep in her throat.

A few minutes later, Richard shook his long tail back and forth. She moaned with pleasure and gritted her teeth in his flesh. Nuts touch his chin with every stroke. He liked how his huge tail lengthened his jaw. Elizabeth loves to suck dick but realizes that she loves to suck dick, Richard. "Well, you can stop now," he said. "Lighten your limbs and bend over the bed," he ordered. "Put your face on the blankets."Yes, sir!" This could not stop when he suddenly squeezed his cock into dripping pussy. He hit her vagina so hard that the young woman could not control herself. Elizabeth began to boil and scream so loudly that Richard was sure that the neighbors were listening, but he did not care. His cock so wonderfully fills her pussy, and he moved her hands to pull her breasts up when she grabbed the sheets to keep her balance. He slowly lowered his hand between her hips and began to rub her clit.

"Ahhhh !" Named after he began tossing his long dick. "Honey, I'm sorry if I'm cruel, but I have long dreamed, and now I need this cat," he has said the young woman. "I don't cry because it hurts, but because your cock stretches my tight pussy so well!" "Oh, I understand," Richard answered, looking at his white juice above his cock. "Little whore, you painted my dick!" He said. "You are hungry for this meat, right?" she asked, withdrawing her approval. "It's great because you get a lot while you are here!" "Oh yes, give it to me!" "Please fuck my pussy with your big dick," he continued, beating her. "Yes!" When he returned, he cried about another event. "That's all, honey, I understand!" This is it! He cried and allowed him to kneel before him.

"Hey, go under a hard neck, and don't miss a drop!" He orders, pulling sperm into his mouth, and Elizabeth tries to digest everything. His sperm was so thick that he nearly drowned, but was starving because he did not want to disappoint his father's best friend. "On Monday, I want to go to the clinic in the morning and take pills," he said. "Next time I shoot my sperm in your soft, tight pussy," he continued. "Sorry, I mean, my sweet, tight pussy," he added with a smile. "Yes, sir," he answered without rest. The next morning, Elizabeth was already there and have breakfast and to the best friend of her father for. He thought that an elderly person needs food in order to restore his energy, because they had an evening. Richard fell down the stairs in jeans and barefoot, whiles the smell of hot coffee, toast, eggs and lard propelled him. "Hello, tiger," he chirped. "I thought we could discuss what happened last night while we ate, okay?" He said. "I like the smell," he replied. "I can't deny a delicious breakfast," he added without eye contact. She stopped cooking and brought food to the kitchen table. He returned for coffee and tried to keep the atmosphere open. When he sat down, he was her father's best friend saying how much they used the night before and how happy he was to wait all these years. He wanted to tell Richard how long he had dreamed, but the older man had a different vision. "Honey, I'll start," she and Elizabeth nodded to the table, lighting her face with sunlight through the kitchen window.

The young woman felt that things were going badly. "Darling, what happened between us last night was wrong," he began. "We didn't have to do this because I was my father's best friend," he said. "She was always like a girl to me, and I don't want to hurt you," she said. "You are still young all your life," he continued. "You can find any boy there, it's wrong," he added, not convincing. She was nervous when she looked at Elizabeth, when she saw a shell in her heart. "Richard, listen," Elizabeth said. The young woman did not know why her feelings and thoughts disappeared so quickly. "I love you," he said. "After what happened between us last night, I felt like you were the same," he continued. "If you were not a good liar last night, you have feelings for me," he said. "I cannot believe that your relationship with my father or my age prevents us from being together," he continued. "Richard, signs of love are burning, love is unpredictable and unfair, but you cannot control it, you cannot stop it," he said. "What happened last night was the best in my life, please don't take it from me," he complained, standing and standing between his legs, hoping that he would understand his feelings. She hugged her father's best friend and pressed her head to her chest. Richard felt her hard breasts in his silk dress. The tall man screamed in silence. He knelt between his hips and looked carefully at the mature man. Richard stops before he finally speaks. "You are magnificent, and it's hard for this person to say no," he answered, pushing before continuing. "Suppose I

agree to see what we think your parents have?" He asked.

"Your father will kill me without hesitation!" He said.

"Honey, I don't give a damn about death for you, but what do

your parents say?" He asked. "I know what's important to

you, and you cannot always hide," said he. "I am sure that

you want to attend your wedding, your house will look like,

how you want to meet with her husband and children," he

continued. "He said that marriage and children would appear

soon, but you should think about it," he said. "I love you, but

I don't want to hurt you," she admitted. , Elizabeth could not

stop the tears, because the words of Richard were not only

the most enjoyable, what he heard, but also brought they

back to reality. We need to think about his parents and find a

way to convince her of feelings. "Richard, I dreamed so

came last night, I was a teenager," revealed. "I am in love

and wish you more than ten years." He said that "no one can

make me ill while in a casual young man," said he. "I know

that my father is not crazy. I will not kill you," he continued. "If you are worried about my happiness, we accept," he said. "We do not see our love, but we can work together, please," he asked. Richard paused for a few minutes as he spoke. "You're right, I love you, and I love you next to me, nothing else matters to me," she replied, grabbing her face and mistaking her for a passionate kiss. He lowered his hands and grabbed his cheek. Then he dropped his hands under the cloak and slowly pulled it out to expose his body with hungry eyes. Elizabeth leaned forward for a full kiss and ran her fingers through her hair before stroking her tanned breasts. His upper body was very masculine, and each muscle was ready to explode through the skin.

Richard looked at the young woman with his brown eyes, pulled her hard nipples hard, and released one to grab her teeth. Elizabeth came in, and the smell made the air thicker.

She groans with pleasure as her father's best friend lifts her breasts and bites her. When she teased her nipples, she lowered her hand and banged hard before he started playing with her pussy. He gave his juice to her pussy lips and left her nipples before looking at her. "I love you," he said. "I love you more than anything," he replied with a smile. "It was hard for you last night, but I want to examine your body slowly," she said, lifting her and hugging her waist. She began to kiss his neck, putting it on. He took her to his room and carefully laid her on the bed.

Elizabeth slowly reached out and gradually extended her legs to show her reward. Her fingers licked before chewing her breasts. Then he used his other hand to nibble on her clitoris. "Richard, what are you waiting for? Take off your clothes with me," he said playfully. He took off his jeans and shorts before going to bed. He removed his fingers from his chest and kissed the inside of his thigh before slipping into his lips. Of course, before you lick, and this happens every time you clean a swollen clitoris. She put both hands on balloons and began to play with hard nipples, while her best friend's father made her pussy happy. Seconds later, he started in and out of her pussy to the crease, because he loved the delicious liquid that her body made him comfortable. Elizabeth picked up the blanket and tucked away her chest. She held her breath for a while to prepare for the most intense peak in oral form was sex. Richards looked happily between his folded legs.

"Oh Richard, yes, yes, he cried explosively, his upper one began to disappear, and her father's best friend kissed her body and thoughts of her breast for a while: "Baby if you want, I need you desperately, as he lifted the head. "Not now," he replied in a loud voice, biting his neck before sliding over one of her breasts. Richard knew this region to stimulate an experienced language. This stimulation attracted a young woman when she pressed a hard cock to her tight pussy. Elizabeth complained loudly and immediately kicked the old man as he squeezed his fatty meat and went out. Outside, it was difficult, and for everything that he felt before, his huge instrument and curves extend deep, enjoying every second of them will be attacked, gently pulled on his hair, so that "he took off his left hand on his left foot in press g the best access to keep them restrained him and nailed him behind her while they continued to lick her pussy. A tall man an incision in his neck and scratched it. "Run for me, dear," called him to. Elizabeth gave him everything she had. He held her with joy and grabbed his cock because he felt closer to that moment than in the past and loved her. Richard caught him and Elizabeth felt his cock grow in her. I knew that a big man would explode. "Tax, it's now your turn, run after me," he insisted. "Dad, fill my pussy, shoot my cum, I want it to flow on my ass," he added. His dirty speech was too persuasive for him when he exploded violently inside and threw his big eggs into his chain. Then he turned and sat next to him. She smiled at him. "Hey, it was a fantastic breakfast," he said. He laughed, looking at him, and stood up the stairs to hug. She gently wore her lips. "Why don't we watch the movie after the shower?" "Good," he replied. They both went to the bathroom.

Dirty Daddies

Sex with the Big Black11 Inch Cock

It was an unfortunate and tedious day at work. The most unpleasant thing is that your desire to refuel has increased. I was recently ready for me as a bitch. I was expecting something that I could not explain. I still needed a real member. I wanted to open my mouth and enjoy the hot cum on the lips that flowed down my throat. I put on my favorite white long-necked blouse, tight skirt, black socks, and high heels. He was blond, tall, with large sexy breasts, a thin body, and long legs. But I never had panties there, since I was a student, the student did not like this type of clothing for women. On my way back, I came to a sex shop, not far from my house. When I entered the store, a wave of emotions struck me. Six people went through windows and forests to look at magazines and objects on shelves. Everyone turned to me and looked at me as a celebrity. I assumed that I would kneel and suck it. I was sure that these guys never saw girls like me in this store. "I wonder if everyone wanted to sleep with me." This thought crossed my mind, and I was very excited. I went to the game department and, for a while, looked at anal and vaginal vibrators, lubricants, and leather handles.

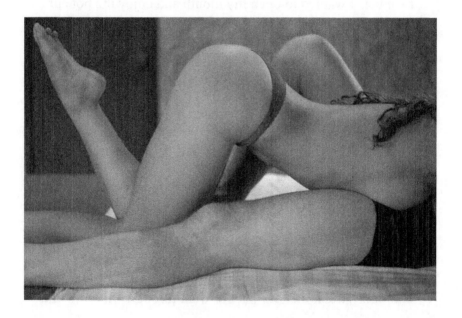

Finally, I went in and went to the seller: he noticed that my hands were trembling when I paid. I saw a smile on his lips, and he seemed to guess what was happening with this shaker. I got into my car and decided to have fun with this game. I forgot to buy a lubricant, so I chose a face cream. I opened my legs to put it in the anus; it was tight, inch by inch, because there was a narrow hole. After I inserted it, he took me out of the car and returned to the store. Every step I took was happy. It was so good to follow him. I again contacted the seller and asked him for marks that give free access to all video cabins. She smiled at the Sphinx and gave me three ratings. I thanked him and went to the video section. Some children come, take a taxi and close the door. Each cabin had a particular hole in the wall on the right side of the seat. Suddenly a light appeared in this hole, thinking that someone was going to a neighboring house to relax. I put a stamp on the slot machine, and there was a porn movie. There, a girl blew up a boy. I looked at the hole on the right and saw a neighbor staring at me. He rolled his eyes in shame, but he knew something that he would never believe. I have to be a real bitch and suck someone tonight. I pushed back the chair and knelt before this hole. The floor was dirty and saliva. The man looked behind me, opened when his fly, and pulled out his penis and put it in the hole for me. I heard a noise in the next taxi on the left and suspected that someone wanted to spy on me.

I played on this member, slowly put it in my mouth and held my tongue together. Her erection did not immediately undermine my efforts, but she was quickly set up. We heard the man moaning loudly and panting. He hurried closer to the wall so that I sucked his cock deeper. He arrived promptly, a few minutes after launch. Complete it and leave it behind. But that was not enough for me, so I leaned over and checked another hole. Another boy was sitting in a chair, masturbating. I knew that he had seen me hit this guy, and my excitement intensified. He went to the wall and squeezed his cock into the hole. I immediately went downstairs and took my vulgar mouth as deep as possible. I wanted to kiss my mouth! I stuck to the wall, so my nose played on the wall, my lips crossed the penis that was supposed to come. I made one of the dirty foxes, and each of them wanted to suck, and their mouths were nothing more than a can of sperm, but the only place I could get. This guy increased his speed and started fucking me faster and faster. His cock looked into my mouth to grow; his balls hit me on the chin every time he hit me on the penis. It was the best that I would die inside your sperm.

I wanted to be treated like a street girl with a low-quality skirt. In the end, his cock got more prominent, and sperm filled my mouth. He ran under his chin and slipped into my shirt. Shortly after someone knocked on my taxi door, I entered the castle and left it behind. Big black came up. She looked at me and smiled. Then he opens the jeans and begins a big black cock, 30 cm long, so big and fat that I started. Insert my lips into this phallus was not easy, although I quickly succeeded and began to move my head in rhythm. But he grabbed my head and let me move as soon as possible. I was often sick and had difficulty vomiting. Although he didn't care, he whispered to me: "Come on, bitch, does it! Take it all, bitch! With his right hand, he lifted my blouse and stroked my breasts. He jerked his cock from time to time and beat me with it. "Tell me what you want, bitch, cake!" And I'll do something like "yes." "Drink here, suck me, and bitch!"I knew what I was thinking, and it's true, he grabbed my head and continued to kiss my hard mouth, the deeper and crueler head of state put me in the throat, tears flowed from my eyes, but didn't want any tomato flavor. I looked up and was satisfied that little - by and by, I was the curve of the street's low cost! I knew that the people who listen to suck me, I don't worry, because I would like to hear my rap and break. I would like to know what I did in the salon. She, I saw him throw into the eyes of a nearby taxi, and I was thrilled.

My strong desire increased when this black guy struck me and fast. He quickly leaned against the wall, and I realized that I was ready to come. My heart melted with joy when it came into my mouth with a mighty, innocent oath. Cum melts in your mouth and fills everything. Some fell on my cheeks. He interrupted me and wiped my face, and then ordered me to lick everything, obeyed. Without saying anything, he left me and left me alone in my lap. Leave the door open so that everyone can see how good and cheap it was. Finally, I recovered and went to the entrance. My hair was tangled, I saw dirty traces of sperm on my socks, and my skirt and blouse were not buttoned. I knew that all the shoppers in the store were looking at me and knew what had just happened in the salon. This is the core of my rhythm with enthusiasm and the realization that everyone knows that I am a whore who loves beats. I knew it was right, and it was a cake, and my mouth was for suctioning, and that was the only thing I liked the most.

Dirty Daddies

The End

Thanks for reading. Please put a valuable review and wait for the next one